KNIGHTMARE
Foul Play!

PETER BENTLEY

Stripes

CEDRIC'S WORLD

CASTLE BOMBAST

Sir Percy the Proud

Cedric
Thatchbottom
(Me!)

Patchcoat the Jester

Margaret the Cook

For Lucy, T...

STRIPES PUBLISHING
An imprint of Little Tiger Press
1 The Coda Centre, 189 Munster Road,
London SW6 6AW

A paperback original
First published in Great Britain in 2015

Text copyright © Peter Bently, 2015
Cover illustrations copyright © Fred Blunt, 2015
Illustrations copyright © Artful Doodlers, 2015

ISBN: 978-1-84715-612-9

The right of Peter Bently and Artful Doodlers to be identified
as the author and illustrator of this work respectively has been
asserted by them in accordance with the Copyright, Designs and
Patents Act, 1988.

Printed and bound in the UK.

10 9 8 7 6 5 4 3 2 1

BLACKSTONE FORT

Sir Roland the Rotten

Walter Warthog

SPIFFINGTON MANOR

Algernon Whympleigh

Sir Spencer the Splendid

Chapter One
Flock Block

HISS!

"Come along, Cedric. Hurry up and shift them!"

"I'm trying my best, Sir Percy!"

I flapped my arms at the flock of geese blocking the road. "Shoo! Shoo!"

The birds didn't budge. They just stood there, eyeing me suspiciously.

A large crowd was building up on the
road behind us. Then a bunch of youths,
all wearing white and dark blue scarves,
started chanting, "*Why are we wai-ting?
Why-y are we waiting?*"

KNIGHTMARE

I glanced back at my master. "Er, you could always ride *around* the geese, Sir Percy," I suggested. "We could catch up with you at the fair."

"Don't be ridiculous, Cedric," said Sir Percy. "A knight cannot be seen arriving at a major public event without – um – an *entourage*. It simply isn't *done*, dear boy."

To most knights an entourage means an impressive following of smartly dressed soldiers, plus maybe a trumpeter and a page or two carrying banners with the knight's coat of arms. To Sir Percy it meant me, Patchcoat the jester and Margaret the cook, riding on a rickety cart pulled by Gristle, the old mule.

KNIGHTMARE

We were on our way to the May Fair at Blodger's Bottom – a village not far from Castle Bombast where the kingdom's four main roads met. The May Fair was the biggest market of the year, and villagers and peasants came from all over the kingdom to sell their wares. Better still, Patchcoat had told me there were minstrels, morris dancers, a maypole, and all sorts of other fun and games – including the Mad Maze, which was so fiendishly difficult people got lost in it for hours on end.

Patchcoat said there was also a big five-a-side football tournament called the May Fair Trophy. I was really looking forward to that, as I used to love kicking a ball around

with my friends before I came to work for
Sir Percy. But my master said football was
a horrid peasant pastime, so that was the
end of that.

"Bother these geese," said Sir Percy
impatiently. "At this rate we won't be at the
fair until past lunchtime. And I'm feeling
rather peckish."

Just then, a peasant came shambling
out of the crowd behind us. He was
carrying a tray of shapeless brown lumps
in little sackcloth pouches.

"Did I hear 'ee say 'ee was 'ungry, Yer
Knightship?" he said, holding up the tray.
"I'm just on me way to the fair. Care to try
one o' me snacks?"

"Excellent timing, my good man," said Sir Percy. "Don't mind if I do." He leaned down from Prancelot and took a brownish lump from one of the little sacks. He popped it in his mouth and started to chew.

"*Mmnnnhh* – interesting," he said. He swallowed his mouthful – and instantly burst into a violent fit of coughing.

"Are you all right, Sir Percy?" I asked in alarm.

"HACK! HACK! HACK! – I'm – HACK! HACK! – fine, dear boy – HACK!" he spluttered. His coughing fit finally died down and he shook his head vigorously. "Something seems to have tickled my throat, that's all."

"Oh, that'll be the legs," the peasant grinned, flashing his single tooth.

"*Legs*, my dear fellow?"

"Arrr," said the peasant. "Best bit of a deep-fried cockroach, if 'ee asks me. Wanna buy a bagful, Yer Knightship?"

Sir Percy went green and swayed slightly in the saddle. "Er – no thank you, my good man." Then he belched so loudly it startled the geese. They turned round and hissed.

"Suit yerself, Yer Knightship," said the peasant, disappointed. He wandered back into the crowd, hollering, "Tasty snacks! Tasty snacks! Farthin' a bag!" as he went.

"Deep-fried cockroaches?" snorted Margaret. "That's disgusting!"

"Ew! Too right!" said Patchcoat.

"Yeah," said Margaret. "They're much better grilled."

Now, it would be a *bit* unkind to call Margaret the worst cook in the kingdom. So let's just say she's easily in the bottom two. As far as Margaret's concerned, *haute cuisine* is just a fancy name for porridge.

At that moment another peasant

appeared from behind a nearby bush, waving a staff with one hand and fastening his belt with the other.

"Sorry to keep 'ee waiting, Yer Knightliness," he said cheerily. "Right, let's get you girls off to the fair!" The peasant tapped the rearmost goose on the rump with his staff. It gave a HONK! and the whole flock instantly started to move.

"At last!" said Sir Percy. "On we go!"

I clambered back into the cart next to Patchcoat. He flicked Gristle's reins and we rattled off after my master.

"I can't wait to see the fair!" I said.

"Lucky that messenger showed up when he did, eh, Ced?" said Patchcoat.

15

"You bet!" I agreed. "Otherwise I'd have
been stuck at the castle all day."

Until that very morning Sir Percy
had refused point blank to go to the fair.
He claimed it was terribly *undignified*
for knights to mix with a great mass
of peasants. Patchcoat thought that
sounded suspicious, because *loads* of
knights and other posh folk went to the
May Fair to join in the fun and pick up
a few bargains from the stalls. Not even
the idea of seeing morris dancers could
change his mind – and I *knew* Sir Percy
liked morris dancing because a travelling
troupe had called at Castle Bombast a
few weeks earlier. My master had merrily

clapped along to the dance just like the rest of us.

The worst thing was that servants could have the day off for the May Fair. So Margaret and Patchcoat were allowed to go, but Sir Percy had insisted that *squires* didn't count. After all, he said, *someone* had to stay behind to cook his meals and do all the chores.

I'd been feeling pretty glum when the others were all getting ready to leave that morning. But Patchcoat was just hitching up the mule cart when a messenger came galloping into the courtyard with an urgent scroll for Sir Percy. My master went as white as a sheet when he read it.

Dear Nephew,

I have an appointment today near Castle Bombast so I will be calling in for lunch. It had better be a good one, not like that horrible cabbagey slop you had the nerve to serve me the last time. And you'd better lay on some decent entertainment. I do NOT want to hear any of your ridiculous tall tales about bashing dragons and capturing castles. And if that jester tells me any of his rotten jokes, I'll box your ears. Just like last year.

Your Affectionate Aunt,
Lady Hilda Matilda de Bluster de Bombast

KNIGHTMARE

Whatever had put my master off the fair before, it was obviously nothing compared to a visit from his aunt. He suddenly realized that it would be *most* selfish of him to deprive so many peasants of the chance to see a famous knight. Half an hour later I'd strapped him into his best armour, saddled Prancelot, fetched the threepence my mum and dad had sent me for my birthday, and leaped into the mule cart beside the others.

As we carried on along the road to Blodger's Bottom, we were joined by more and more people heading for the fair. It was

slow going, but everyone was in jolly spirits.
And I definitely wasn't the only one looking
forward to the football. The youths behind
us started waving their scarves and singing
loudly.

Little Piddling,
Little Piddling,
Little Piddling are the best!
We'll be ta-king home the tro-phy
When we've beaten all the rest!

KNIGHTMARE

Beside us was a cart festooned with
the red and white scarves and banners of
a rival team. The five burly farmhands
glowered and suddenly struck up the same
tune, but with rather different words.

I'm a cowpat,
I'm a cowpat,
I'm a cowpat, yes I am!
But I'd rather be a cowpat
Than a Little Piddling fan!

A wave of raucous laughter ran through the crowd.

"Well, really!" huffed Sir Percy. "Thank goodness we shan't be going anywhere near that rowdy lot. Whatever happens, I shall *certainly* be steering clear of the football."

My heart sank.

"Never mind, Ced," Patchcoat muttered sympathetically. "There's loads of other things to enjoy."

As he spoke, we reached the top of a low hill. From there we could see four roads packed with people, all streaming into a small village next to a green. Not that you could see much of the green, because most of it was covered with a sea of tents and

22

stalls and animal pens. In the middle of
it all stood a maypole, its bright ribbons
fluttering in the breeze.

"Welcome to Blodger's Bottom!" grinned
Patchcoat.

We had arrived at the fair.

Chapter Two

Morris
Malarkey

What with the crowds heading into the
village from all directions, it took us nearly
half an hour to reach the green. The whole
fairground was ringed by an avenue
of poles from which colourful banners
fluttered brightly. I assumed the poles were
just for decoration, but when we reached
the outer ring, our way was barred by a

po-faced peasant with a little moustache and a big badge saying "Steward". He had just waved through the cart with the five farmhands, who were still merrily singing their football chant.

"Wait 'ere a minute, Yer Honour," said the steward, holding up his hand.

"Wait?" said Sir Percy. "Don't be absurd, my dear fellow. I am a knight of the realm. I may go where I please. Kindly step aside."

The steward pursed his lips and frowned as Sir Percy rode a couple of metres past the outer ring of poles. Then, to our left, I noticed a dusty cloud in the middle of the avenue of poles. It was moving with great

25

speed towards my master. Amid the dust
I made out ten men, jostling, kicking and
grabbing each other in an attempt to get
control of – a football!

"Um – Sir Percy," I said. "I think you'd better—"

Before I could finish there was a loud cheer and a THOCK! as one of the footballers got his boot to the ball and cannoned it right past the end of Prancelot's nose.

With a whinny of alarm, Prancelot reared up, nearly tipping Sir Percy out of the saddle. His visor slammed shut, muffling his squawks as he desperately tried to regain his balance. He finally managed to yank himself upright and pull Prancelot back behind the line of poles, just as the footballers thundered past, followed by a handful of cheering supporters.

"I *told* 'ee to wait, Yer Honour," said the steward smugly. "Them poles marks the football course. Now, let's see yer permit."

Sir Percy pushed up his visor. "*Permit?*" he said, flustered. "Now what are you going on about, man?"

"No 'orses an' carts in the fair without a permit," said the steward. "Too crowded, see."

KNIGHTMARE

"But that's ridiculous," huffed Sir Percy. He pointed at the five farmhands in the cart, now disappearing into the crowd. "You let *them* in."

"*They've* got a permit," said the steward. "They're playing in the football tournament. Those *without* permits 'as to park over there." He nodded towards some specially erected railings nearby.

"Oh, very well," sighed Sir Percy. "But this is *most* inconvenient."

As the steward scuttled off to check the permit of a bloke driving a cartload of turnips, Sir Percy dismounted from Prancelot. He held out her reins to me.

"Off you trot, Cedric," he said.

"I shall wait for you here."

"Yes, Sir Percy," I said, clambering from the cart.

Patchcoat hopped down after me. "You may as well park the cart, too, Ced," he grinned. "Seeing as you're going anyway."

"Cheers, Patchcoat," I said. "By the way, what did the steward mean by a football *course*? Don't they play on a proper pitch?"

"The May Fair Trophy is a bit different from other football tournaments," said Patchcoat. "Each match is really more of a *race*. Can get a bit rough sometimes, but it's very entertaining. Sorry you'll miss the fun."

"Me, too," I said. "My chances of slipping off on my own are virtually zilch."

"Anyway, I'll see you later, Ced," said Patchcoat. "I'm off to catch up with some of my jester mates. See if I can try out a few new jokes."

"And I'm off to the Baking Tent," said Margaret, climbing down from the back of the cart. "I reckon I've a good chance of winning that there competition." She nodded at a hoarding advertising events at the fair. Among them was a big poster.

THE GREAT MAY FAIR BAKE OFF

Impress the Judges with Your Pies
And You Could Win a Special Prize!
2pm in the Baking Tent

"Well, your baking will *definitely* make an impression on the judges, Margaret," said Patchcoat, winking at me. "One way or another."

"Oi! Less o' your cheek, Master Patchcoat!" she glowered, shaking her fist.

"Time to go!" chuckled Patchcoat, heading off into the crowd. "See ya later, Ced!"

After tying up Prancelot and Gristle I hurried back to Sir Percy.

"I've parked the animals, Sir Percy," I said politely. "I had to pay a farthing for each of them and another ha'penny for the cart. I don't suppose you could pay me ba—"

KNIGHTMARE

"Later, dear boy, later," Sir Percy said. "If we dawdle any longer, the fair will be over before we've even started. Now, what shall we see first?" I followed him as he strode over to the hoarding. "Aha! The very thing."

To my delight he stopped right in front of a poster about the football tournament.

THE MAY FAIR TROPHY

Annual All-Comers

Five-a-Side Football Tournament

First Match: 10am

Final Match: Whenever there
are only two teams left

Matches start and end at the
Village Church

"I gather it is a most, er, *fascinating* tradition, Cedric," Sir Percy said. "Ancient, too, I shouldn't wonder."

"Er, the football, Sir Percy?" I said in surprise.

"*Football*, Cedric?" he replied. "*That* ruffianly game? Are you trying to be amusing? Certainly not! I am talking about the May Queen Parade."

I followed his gaze and realized he wasn't looking at the football poster at all. He was reading the one right next to it.

ANNUAL MAY QUEEN PARADE
on the Village Green
Fun and Games!
Music and Maypole Dancing!
to celebrate the

CROWNING OF THE MAY QUEEN

KNIGHTMARE

"Come along, Cedric," Sir Percy said, striding off. "I think it would be most – um – *educational* for you to see it."

Not to mention a perfect chance for you to show off in front of a bunch of damsels, I thought.

We jostled our way through the hustle and bustle of the fair, and finally reached the open area of the green by the maypole. A crowd of peasants was standing around expectantly. But there was no sign of any damsels. An empty throne-like chair, engraved with the words "Guest of Honour", stood at a large table.

In the centre of the table was a shiny copper circlet decorated with silver flowers.

To the left of this was an oversized spoon made out of polished brass and mounted on a wooden stand. I guessed they were the May Queen's crown and the prize for the winner of the Great May Fair Bake Off. But it was the third object that really caught my eye. It was a handsome silver cup, engraved with a picture of what was unmistakably a football. The May Fair Trophy! I tried not to think about all the matches I would be missing that day.

"When does the May Queen contest start, my good man?" said Sir Percy to one of the stewards, interrupting my thoughts.

"Oh, not till teatime, Yer Knightship," said the steward. "After the football."

"Then what are all these people waiting for?" asked my master.

"'Ee'll soon see, Yer Knightship," said the steward. "'Ere they come now." There was a jangling sound and a great cheer went up from the crowd. "Make way!" cried the steward. "Make way for the morrismen!"

"Um – morrismen?" Sir Percy went a little pale.

The crowd parted to let through a fiddler, a drummer and a bagpiper, followed by half a dozen guys wearing colourful costumes and bells on their sleeves and trousers. They were all carrying long cudgels.

"Oh look, Sir Percy!" I said. "It's those

morris dancers who came to play at Castle Bombast a few weeks back. They were really good!"

"Come on, Yer Knightship," beamed the steward, dragging Sir Percy by the arm. "I'll get 'ee a good spot."

But Sir Percy seemed rather reluctant to go. "Ah – um – my good man, there's really no need, I, er—"

Before my master could protest any more, the steward had thrust us both right to the front of the crowd. Unfortunately, he thrust a bit too hard, because Sir Percy ended up flailing right into the path of the morris dancers. The chief dancer had to pull up short to avoid a collision.

"Careful, Yer Knightship!" exclaimed
the morrisman. "I nearly— 'Ang on. Don't
I know 'ee?"

My master shook his head. "Good
gracious me no, my dear fellow," he said
innocently. "I am one hundred per cent
certain that I've never seen you before in
my—"

The morrisman cut him off. "'Ere, lads!"
he gasped. "It's that knight! The one that
never paid us! 'E owes us five shillin's!"

So Patchcoat was right! There *was*
another reason why Sir Percy had wanted
to avoid the May Fair.

My master edged towards me. "Um
– Cedric," he hissed out of the side of his
mouth. "I think perhaps we'd better, er,
how can I put this ... RUN!"

With that he swivelled round and

barged back into the crowd at full pelt.

"After 'im, boys!" cried the chief morrisman.

"Oi! What about the dance?" said the steward, as the morrismen raised their cudgels and set off after my master.

"We'll be back in a tick," said the chief morrisman. "Just as soon as we've got our money out of this chiseller!"

"But what if 'e don't cough up?" said the steward.

The chief morrisman grinned. "Well, in that case we'll just 'ave to teach 'im a lesson 'e won't forget," he said. "Cudgels at the ready, lads!"

Yikes! I pushed my way through the crowd just in time to spot Sir Percy's plume bobbing and weaving through the food stalls.

"There 'e is!" yelled one of the morrismen – and promptly ran into a passing peasant wheeling a handcart full of pots and pans. They all clattered to the ground. While the dancers helped to pick them up, I caught a glimpse of my master ducking under the flap of a nearby tent. A few moments later the morrismen were off again. They ran on past the tent and disappeared into the fair.

I hurried to tell my master it was safe to come out – only to hear sudden screams and yelps coming from the tent.

"Help!" screeched a female voice. "There's a bloomin' peepin' Tom in the May Queen Changing Tent! Fetch the stewards!"

A second later Sir Percy scrambled out, followed by a pointy shoe that flew through the air and clanged off his helmet.

"Oof! Ah, there you are, Cedric," he said, speeding off into the crowd as fast as

43

his armour would let him. "Might be best to – um – make ourselves scarce."

As he turned to speak to me, he didn't look where he was going.

"Watch out, Sir Percy!" I yelled.

But it was too late.

TWANG!

BOOF!

Sir Percy had tripped on a guy rope and hurtled headlong into a figure who now lay sprawled on his back in the dust. It was none other than his best friend, Sir Spencer the Splendid.

Chapter Three
Header Hoo-Ha

"Just look at my outfit!" moaned Sir Spencer.

His squire helped him up. "Don't worry,
Sir Spencer," he simpered, pulling a brush
from his pocket and sweeping the dust off
his master. "I'll soon have you looking spick
and span!"

"Thank you, Algernon," said Sir Spencer,
running his fingers through his long golden

locks. "So, Perce, what's the big rush? And what was that shouting all about?"

"Er, nothing, Spence old bean," smiled Sir Percy, with a nervous glance over his shoulder. "Just a slight – um – *misunderstanding*. What's with the outfits?"

Sir Spencer and Algernon were wearing smart new ankle boots, plus splendid gold and green velvet tabards and knee britches with matching stockings. The tabards bore Sir Spencer's emblem of a blazing sun. Behind them were three other men, wearing the same outfits. I recognized two of them as servants of Sir Spencer's, but the third man wasn't familiar at all. Oddly, there seemed to be a faint smell of fish about him.

"The football contest, of course, Perce!"
said Sir Spencer. "We are the Spiffington
Sunbursts. Cool kit, eh? Had it made
especially. Coming to see us win?"

"Football? Certainly not!" said Sir Percy
sniffily. "*Most* unknightly. I've never liked
the game."

"Really?" said Sir Spencer. Then I
saw a mischievous twinkle in his eye.

"But when we were squires you were a brilliant *goalkeeper*, I seem to remember," he chuckled. "Or at least that's what you told your master, eh, Perce? That's why he put you in goal for the knights in that big match against the royal bodyguards. Surely you haven't *forgotten*?"

Sir Percy looked distinctly uncomfortable. Something told me he remembered only too well. "Um – ah, yes," he squirmed. "I really don't think we need to – um – *bore* Cedric here with silly old stories…"

But Sir Percy was wrong. After all his moaning about football, I was *deeply* interested.

Sir Spencer grinned, flashing his brilliant, near-complete set of teeth. "Let me see, how many goals did you let in?" he went on. "Was it twenty-four or twenty-five? We squires called you 'Butterfingers de Bombast' for ages afterwards. Isn't that right, Perce? Ha, ha, ha!"

He clapped Sir Percy on the back so heartily that my master's plume fell out. I managed to grab it before it fluttered into a cauldron of soup on a nearby food stall.

"Hey, nice catch, Frederick!" laughed Sir Spencer. "Pity he wasn't around for that match against the bodyguards, eh, Perce?"

"Um – *most* amusing, Spence," said Sir Percy through gritted teeth.

"Anyway, we'd better get on," said Sir Spencer. "Sure I can't persuade you to come and watch?"

"Er, no thanks, Spence," said Sir Percy. "And by the way, what makes you so sure you'll win?"

"Piece of cake, Perce," grinned Sir Spencer. "It's a simple knockout contest. Whoever wins the match plays the next team, and so on. The team left at the end are the winners. We're sure to face one bunch of weedy peasants after another. Besides, I have a *secret weapon*."

He tapped the side of his nose and nodded at the unfamiliar player. The player gave a rather goofy grin back.

KNIGHTMARE

"His name's Osbertino. Travelling smoked fish merchant by trade." (That explained the fishy whiff.) "He came by Spiffington Manor yesterday, on his way to the fair. Doesn't understand much of what you say to him, but I'm a dab hand at talking to these foreign chaps, Perce. Turns out he was top goalie in his own country. Eh, Osbertino? Best keeper?"

Osbertino nodded eagerly. "Oh yes, *señor* sir! Best keeper in land!"

Sir Spencer cocked an eyebrow. He looked very pleased with himself. "So, with a top-class footballer on our team we're *bound* to end up champions, right?" he said smugly. "See you later, Perce!"

51

Sir Spencer and his team strutted off. The five farmhands we'd seen earlier had looked anything but weedy to me, but hey, perhaps with Osbertino on their team the Spiffington Sunbursts really did stand a chance.

Sir Percy bent down so I could fix his plume back on. As he stood up, a round muddy object suddenly came flying over the surrounding tents.

"Duck, Sir Percy!" I cried.

"A duck, Cedric?" said Sir Percy, straightening up. "Where? OOOF!"

The round object walloped the top of Sir Percy's helmet, crushing his plume before bouncing off into the crowd.

KNIGHTMARE

"Aargh!" cried my master. "Help, Cedric! I'm being attacked by a vicious fowl!"

"It's all right, Sir Percy," I said. "It was only a football."

"That does it!" spluttered Sir Percy. "I'm not spending another minute at this rotten fair. Cedric, we're going home. But first of all I want you to confiscate that wretched ball."

"Yes, Sir Percy," I sighed.

"And while you're about it, get me a cloth," he said. "My armour is all splattered with mud. Ugh!"

I soon found the ball. It had landed in the cauldron of soup. The stallholder stared at me, her face a dripping mask of greyish-green slop.

KNIGHTMARE

"That your ball?" she grunted, nodding at the cauldron.

"Er, well, yes," I replied. "Sort of."

"Take it and clear off," she said.

"Er, thanks," I said and gingerly fished the ball out of the slop. I thought the stallholder was being pretty reasonable, considering. But as I turned to go, she grabbed me by the collar.

"That'll be a penny," she growled. "Fer the wasted soup."

I glumly handed over another chunk of my birthday cash.

KNIGHTMARE

I still had to find Sir Percy a cloth. But
it turned out he didn't need one. He'd been
recognized by some female fans, and several
of them were dabbing the mud off his
armour with their hankies. They were also
bombarding him with questions. I craned
my neck to listen.

"Ooh, Sir Percy, we just saw you
heading that football! Where did you learn
to do that? It was brilliant!" asked one.

"Eh? Oh, um – when I was training to be
a knight," Sir Percy replied. "As a squire I was
renowned for my footballing – um – *prowess*."

That's one way of putting it, I thought.

"Ooh, why ain't you playing today, Sir
Percy?" said another lady.

KNIGHTMARE

"Well, of course I'd *love* to," my master said airily. "But it wouldn't really be fair, would it? What with my footballing skills being so *superior* to everyone else's."

Sir Percy was *really* going off on one. Which usually spelled trouble.

KNIGHTMARE

As if on cue, someone yanked my arm sharply. "Well, well, well! I thought I could *smell* something," sneered a horribly familiar voice. "It's old Fatbottom. *And* he's got our ball. Hand it over!"

I turned to face Walter Warthog, the sneakiest squire in the kingdom. And if Walter was there, his master, Sir Roland the Rotten, couldn't be far away. Sure enough, at that moment Sir Percy's arch-enemy came barging through the crowd.

"Walter, where's that blasted ball?" growled Sir Roland. "We need to get on with our warm-up before the next match. If you don't find it I'll use something else for kicking practice. Like your backside!"

"It's here, Sir Roland," smarmed Walter, snatching the ball from my hands. "*Fatbottom* had it. I expect he was planning to *steal* it, Sir Roland."

"That's not true!" I protested. "Sir Percy just told me to confisc—" I hesitated. If I told Walter and Sir Roland the whole story, my master would be a laughing stock. Now I just had to get Sir Percy to stop showing off.

"Sir Percy!" I called, desperately trying to catch his eye. His fans stopped *ooh*ing and *aah*ing, and turned to stare at me. Unfortunately, Sir Percy just carried on bragging, his eyes closed in rapture.

"Of course, dear ladies, if I *did* play in the football tournament I'd win hands down," he declared. "In fact, I would bet my *whole* castle that I could beat any team at the fair."

Wondering why it had suddenly gone quiet, Sir Percy opened an eye – and found himself staring straight at Sir Roland's fiendish, hairy grin. It was only then that I noticed Sir Roland and Walter were both wearing knee-britches and tabards with Sir Roland's boar's-head emblem. So, too, were the three thick-set, rough-looking blokes who came jogging up behind them.

And then there was that ball…

Uh-oh.

"Meet the Blackstone Fort football team," Sir Roland chuckled. "Me, Walter and three of my toughest castle guards. Percy, I accept your bet. Castle Bombast is as good as mine! Hur-hur-hur!"

Chapter Four
A Twist of Fête

Sir Percy had gone rather pale. "B-b-bet my castle?" he jabbered. "Ha-ha-ha-ha-ha. I th-think you must have *misheard* me, Roly!"

"Really, Percy?" said Sir Roland menacingly. "I could have *sworn* I heard you say you'd win hands down against any team. Isn't that right, ladies?"

"Oh yes!" said one of the ladies. "Sir Percy's just teasing, Your Honour. He's the best footballer in the kingdom!"

"Eh?" Sir Roland snorted. "Who – *him?*"

"That's right!" said the lady. "He's been telling us all about it. How many times did you lead the king's own bodyguards to victory, Sir Percy?"

"Er, my dear lady..." said Sir Percy.

"Now don't be so modest, Sir Percy," said another fan. "Tell him about the record number of goals you scored!"

"Most of them were headers, you know!" piped up another lady.

"And he's a champion goalie!" said another.

KNIGHTMARE

My master looked like he wanted the ground to swallow him up. Sir Roland burst out laughing.

"Well, well, well. So old Butterfingers de Bombast is a champion goalie, is he?" he cackled unpleasantly. "Oh, this match is going to be *such* fun! I hope you've brought the keys to Castle Bombast, Percy. I've always fancied a country cottage. Hur-hur-hur!"

As he spoke, four forlorn figures dressed in filthy rags came staggering past us. One had a grubby bandage around his head. Another was limping along on a crutch. They were covered in cuts and bruises, though it was hard to tell under all the mud.

63

"Poor beggars," I said, opening my purse and taking out one of my last two pennies.

"Don't be stupid, Fatbottom," sneered Walter. "They're not *beggars*. That's the team we've just defeated. Bunch of farmhands, apparently."

Farmhands? Yikes.

"But there are only four of them," I said. "Where's the fifth?"

In answer two stewards appeared carrying a man on a stretcher.

KNIGHTMARE

"Foolish peasant knocked himself out," said Walter. "Dived for the ball and landed head first on Sir Roland's left boot. *Terribly* unlucky, don't you think, Fatbottom?"

"Walter!" bellowed Sir Roland. "Don't just stand there or we'll be late for our next match. Percy, you'd better get your team ready. We've won every match so far and we're running out of opponents. Oh, and by the way," he added, as he stomped off. "Don't forget the Knight's Code of Honour. If you don't show up to play, you'll be going back on your bet. And I'll get your castle anyway! Hur-hur-hur!"

As he turned to follow his master, Walter grinned nastily. "When we *do* move in I'll make sure Sir Roland gets rid of that rotten cook of yours," he hissed. "*And* that terrible jester. But don't worry, Fatbottom, *you* won't have to leave. We'll still need someone to clean the toilets. He-he-he!"

I glared at Walter's retreating back. Then I looked at Sir Percy. He was staring into space with his mouth open, whimpering softly.

"Sir Percy," I said. "What are we going to do?"

My master gave his head a vigorous shake. "Well, whatever happens, I have no intention of letting that lumbering oaf have my castle," he said. "Cedric, you shall simply have to see that Sir Roland loses!"

KNIGHTMARE

"*Me*, Sir Percy?"

Uh-oh. I had a horrible feeling that this chat wasn't going to end well.

"Indeed," said Sir Percy. "It will be an excellent opportunity to acquire some essential leadership skills."

"Er, *what* will be, Sir Percy?"

"Leading Team Bombast to victory, of course," he said. "I hereby appoint you team captain. It's a great honour. Congratulations!"

A great honour? I thought. *A great way of ending up on a stretcher, more like.*

"But Sir Percy," I asked, as politely as I could, "isn't there one slight snag? We don't *have* a team."

"That's where you're wrong, dear boy," he said. "There's you and Patchcoat for starters. Find another three fellows and you're in business."

"Don't you mean *two*, Sir Percy?" I said. "There are already three of us. Including you."

Sir Percy suddenly screwed up his face and gasped. "Aargh! My ankle!" He put out a hand to steady himself against a neighbouring stall. "Ooh! Must've twisted it when I, er, when I tripped over that guy rope."

Yeah, right. Funny how he hadn't mentioned twisting his ankle till now. I guessed what was coming.

68

"My – *ooh!* – dear – *ah!* – Cedric!" Sir Percy went on. "I fear – *ooh!* – it is *highly* unlikely I can – *ouch!* – take part in the match." (Yup. Got it in one.) "Of course I shall – *aaaah!* – be *very* sorry to disappoint all those ladies. Cedric, as captain you will also be responsible for finding the team some kit to wear. I shall take charge of important matters such as – um – strategy, tactics and – and…"

But before he could think of anything else we heard a sound nearby.

Jingling.

"There he is, lads! Oi, you! Armour-features!"

It was the morrismen!

"Er, kindly deal with those gentlemen, would you, Cedric?" Sir Percy said with a look of alarm. "I really ought to go to the, er, First-Aid Tent and – um – get this ankle seen to!"

Luckily for Sir Percy, the morrismen found their way blocked by a passing peasant pushing a handcart piled high with brass chamber pots. Sir Percy crouched behind the handcart and scuttled off out of sight – just in the nick of time.

"Right, where's that blinkin' master of yours?" said the chief morrisman, running up and shaking his fist under my nose.

"S-sorry, gents," I said nervously. "Y-you just missed him. He went – that way!"

I pointed in the opposite direction from the handcart. (Mind you, after the way Sir Percy had just landed me in it, I was sorely tempted to send them straight after him.)

"Bother," said the chief morrisman, eyeing me suspiciously. "Right, sonny. We've got to go and do a show. But when you see yer master, tell 'im 'e's not goin' to escape a third time. Is that clear?"

"Er, yes, very clear!" I said.

"Good," said the chief morrisman. "Right, come on, lads!"

As the morrismen turned and headed back in the direction of the maypole, I spotted Sir Percy dashing from the cover of the handcart straight into a large pavilion. I'd never seen anyone with a twisted ankle (and wearing a suit of armour) move with such *incredible* speed. And, for that matter, I'd never come across a First-Aid Tent with a big sign outside saying "Refreshments".

Chapter Five
Scream Team

"He did WHAT?" Patchcoat almost dropped the pasty he was eating.

"It's true," I said. "*And* if he backs out of the bet he'll be disgraced."

"But we'll be massacred!" said Patchcoat. "*And* we'll end up homeless into the bargain. Nice one, Sir Percy!"

I'd found Patchcoat sitting on a bench in

front of a makeshift stage where one jester after another was getting up and telling their latest gags.

"Oi, shh, will you?" said the man next to us. "I'll miss the punchline!"

Patchcoat and I stopped talking while the jester onstage cracked his next joke.

"I say, I say, I say!" he said. "What do you call a man with a plank of wood on his 'ead? *Edward!*"

There were a few titters.

"And what do you call a man with *two* planks on his 'ead? I dunno – but *Edward would*! Geddit?"

The audience cracked up. But I wasn't in much of a mood for laughing.

74

KNIGHTMARE

"Hold on," said Patchcoat suddenly. "It's a knockout contest, right?"

I nodded.

"That means we only have to play Sir Roland if his team keeps winning, right?"

"Right."

"So what if someone beats him *before* we have to play?"

"What, like Sir Spencer?" I said. "Maybe. He's got some top foreign player on his team. But Sir Roland's lot will be a tough team to beat."

I described what had happened to the farmhands.

"Hmm. Good point," said Patchcoat. "But cheer up, Ced. I'm sure we'll think of something. In the meantime, there's no point sitting around here moping."

"I suppose you're right," I sighed. "If we don't show up at all then Sir Percy will lose his bet anyway. But I have no idea where we're going to find *three* more players *and* get some football kit before the match!"

"Well, we might as well go and find a spot to have a practice anyway," said Patchcoat. "Maybe we'll come up with a plan on the way."

"Hold on," I said. "Don't you need to have your turn telling jokes first?"

"Er, no," said Patchcoat. "I've already been."

"Oh right," I said. "How did it go?"

KNIGHTMARE

"Not too bad, actually," Patchcoat smiled, brushing a bit of turnip peeling off his tunic. "Some of the stuff they chucked was actually *fresh*."

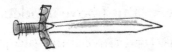

We found a patch of open ground between the poultry enclosure and the Baking Tent, and not far from the Mad Maze, a huge wooden circular enclosure with sides that towered high above my head and only one very narrow entrance. (Patchcoat wasn't exaggerating when he said it was tricky. I could see quite a few people going in, but no one coming out.)

As we passed the Baking Tent Margaret

came out, fanning her red sweaty face with a wooden spoon. "Phew!" she said. "Just popped out for a breath of fresh air. It's like an oven in there!"

"Maybe something to do with all the – ovens?" said Patchcoat.

Margaret pursed her lips. "Very funny, Master Patchcoat," she said. "You won't be laughin' when you see my Showstopper cake. It'll blow your mind!"

"Not to mention my guts," muttered Patchcoat. He dodged behind me to avoid a swipe of the wooden spoon.

KNIGHTMARE

"Sorry, Margaret," I said. "But we need to start practising. The thing is, we're in a bit of a pickle." I explained about the match.

Margaret frowned. "Three more players? Well, I'd 'elp if I could, Master Cedric, but I need to be here for the judging of the Bake Off," she said. "'Course, if Sir Roland wins 'e's sure to keep *me* on at the castle. But I'd 'ate to see you two out on the street."

Patchcoat raised an eyebrow.

"'Ere, I know!" she said suddenly. "I'll ask me brother Ham!"

"*Brother?*" I said.

"Aye," said Margaret. "Bumped into him just after I left you. He's over there with me two nephews."

We followed Margaret's gaze to see a muscular shepherd chatting to two younger lads. Each was carrying a shaggy sheep around his shoulders.

"There you go, Ced," said Patchcoat. "With blokes like that on our side we might even stand a chance!"

We went after Margaret as she waddled toward the strapping shepherds — and walked straight past them to a skinny peasant sitting on a haybale, slurping out of a flagon. Next to him sat two spotty youths, who were only a couple of years older than me. One was busy picking things out of his hair and examining them closely. The other (who was a lot plumper and bore a striking resemblance to his aunt) was scoffing an enormous pork pie.

"Orright, brother Ham? Orright, Botolph and Godwit?" said Margaret.

"Orright, Auntie Maggie!" said the youths together.

"Orright, sis," beamed her brother. "We just sold the last of our ducks. Fancy a drop o' mead to celebrate?"

"No thank, 'ee, brother," said Margaret.
"But I'm glad you sold yer ducks because
Sir Percy needs you lot in his football team.
Ain't that right, Master Cedric?"

"Football, sis?" said Ham uncertainly.
"I ain't so sure about that. It's a long while
since I last played…"

The two nephews looked at him in
surprise.

Something tiny and black that Botolph
was holding between his thumb and
forefinger took the chance to leap back
on to his head. "What, Pa? Did 'ee play
football?" he said.

"'Ee never told us that!" said Godwit,
spraying pie down his chin.

KNIGHTMARE

"Your pa don't like to talk about it," said Margaret. "But he captained the Great Blustering Duck Breeders' Apprentices. Won the May Fair Trophy three times. Ain't that right, brother?"

"Arrh," said Ham. "We was unstoppable. Till that incident with the slurry pit."

"What happened?" I asked.

"The course was a bit different then," said Ham. "Me and the lads went chargin' off, wondering why the other team were bein' so slow. Soon found out. Part of the course involved runnin' over a slurry pit across some planks. Turns out *someone* had sawn through 'em. All five of us fell in."

I couldn't help myself from gasping. "Ew!"

"Course, we lost," said Ham. "Took us an hour to get out, and nobody would come near any of us for a month. Couldn't bring meself to play after that."

"But if 'ee don't play, brother, Sir Roland will get Castle Bombast," said Margaret.

"Sir Roland?" said Ham. "Why didn't 'ee say so, sis! That's different, that is."

"Why's that, Pa?" said Godwit.

"The team that beat us in the slurry game was a bunch of young squires. Captained by a certain *Roland* de Blackstone."

"Sir Roland!" Patchcoat and I exclaimed together.

"The very same!" said Ham. "Well, maybe it's finally time to brush up me dribbling skills. I'm a bit rusty, mind."

"Nice one, brother," said Margaret. "Right, I'm off back to the Baking Tent to get me cake out of the oven. See you later, and good luck!"

Ham turned to his two sons. "Right, boys, you up fer it?" he said.

"Erm, you only have to play if you *want* to, of course," I chipped in.

"You bet, Master Cedric!" said the pie-scoffing youth. "'Ow about you, Botty?"

"Oh arrh!" said Botolph. "Us has always wanted to play football."

"Um – you have actually *played* before, haven't you?" I asked.

"'Course," said Godwit, displaying a

85

mouthful of half-chewed pie. "It's that game where you wallops a ball over a net."

"That ain't football, Goddo, you numbskull!" said Botolph, plucking something from his scalp and popping it into his mouth. "That's *hockey*. Football's the one where you rolls a ball to knock over some sticks."

"Um – I think we might need to put in a tiny bit of practice," I said.

"There's something else we need first, Ced," said Patchcoat. "A football."

"I saw some for sale in that tent over there," said Ham. "I reckon they might lend us one for a quick kickabout."

"Thanks, Ham!" I said.

KNIGHTMARE

I dashed off through the crowds to a
big tent that said "Foreign Goods". Just by
the entrance was what looked like a whole
stall of footballs. The stallholder – a large
woman in a brightly checked dress and a
matching cap with a bobble on top – was
busy serving a customer and had her back
to me. While I was waiting, I picked up a
ball to try it for bounce. It felt a bit heavy,
but I tossed it on to my foot and gave it a
hefty kick.

SPLURGH!

To my horror, the ball burst all over my
foot in a squishy brownish mass of mush.
It looked a bit like porridge. Porridge mixed
with chopped giblets.

KNIGHTMARE

The stallholder spun round. "Hey! What d'ye think yer up to, laddie? That was one o' ma finest haggises!"

"Um – sorry, missus," I said, still staring at my besplattered foot.

"*Missus?* How dare ye!"

I looked up. Whoops. Now he'd turned round I could see that the stallholder was most definitely a bloke. It was the flaming red beard that clinched it.

"S-sorry, sir," I said. "You see, I saw your dress, and I thought—"

"*Dress?*" he boomed. "It's a kilt, ye cheeky wee beggar! And that'll be a ha'penny fer the haggis."

I reluctantly handed over my last penny, pocketed the ha'penny change and beat a hasty retreat. My birthday cash had almost gone and I still hadn't found a football.

"Oi! Mind out!" A peasant pushing a large barrow pulled up short just in time to avoid squishing me.

"Eek!" I said. "Sorry, I was miles away."

I stood aside as the barrow boy shook his head and carried on his way.

And then I noticed what the barrow was

89

laden with. They were round, just the right size and unlikely to explode when kicked…

"Excuse me!" I said, running after the barrow. "How much are your cabbages?"

Chapter Six

Kickabout Catastrophe

Armed with a pair of cabbages, the five of us made for the clearest part of the patch of open ground, close to the poultry enclosure. Three tumblers were performing some impressive acrobatics nearby, but there was still plenty of room for a kickabout.

"All we need now is a goal," I said, after I'd scraped the haggis off my foot.

I spotted a pile of empty sacks near a long table outside the Baking Tent. "Ah! We can use a couple of those."

"I wonder what was in them?" said Patchcoat, picking one up.

"Well," I said. "They're next to the Baking Tent so I'd guess they're—"

Before I could finish, Patchcoat gave the sack a good shake. I was instantly engulfed in a great white cloud.

"Flour sacks," I said, coughing. "Cheers, Patchcoat!"

"What's up, Ced?" he giggled. "You've gone as white as a sheet."

"Very funny," I said, shaking flour out of my hair. I brushed myself down and grabbed a couple of sacks to use as goal markers.

"Hold on, Ced, I've just had an idea," said Patchcoat. He held one of the sacks up against himself. "Hmm. Perfect length. Just need to make three holes…" He tore apart a bit of the seams on three sides of the sack, then pulled the whole thing over his head. "Ta-da! That's our kit sorted. What d'you reckon?"

"Er, not exactly *professional*," I laughed. "But I suppose it's better than nothing."

Once Patchcoat had kitted us all out, we started to give Botolph and Godwit some footballing tips.

"I gather the May Fair tournament isn't what you'd call a *normal* game of football," I said. "But the basic idea is the same, right, Ham?"

"That's right, young master," said Ham. "In this match we have to chase the ball on a course around the whole fair, starting and finishing at the church. The church porch is the goal. First team to get the ball into the porch wins."

"So let's practise getting the ball into the goal," I said, placing a cabbage on the ground. "You can move the ball forward in any way you like. Obviously it goes further if you *kick* it. But you can head it or throw it, too. Is that clear?"

"I reckon so, Master Cedric," said Botolph, scratching his head.

"Easy peasy, Master Cedric!" said Godwit, munching one last bit of pie crust.

"Right, I'll go first, and you try and stop me getting it in goal," I said.

I gave the cabbage a kick towards the goal. As it rose into the air, Godwit waddled backwards to try and catch it, but didn't look where he was going and crashed into Botolph. As they fell in a heap, the cabbage sailed over the goal — and landed slap-bang in the middle of one of the goose pens.

"I'll get it," I sighed.

The gooseherd we'd met on our way to the fair was leaning on the fence.

"Excuse me," I said. "Do your geese bite?"

"No, young master," said the gooseherd.

Relieved, I clambered over the fence and carefully stepped among the honking horde. I bent down to pick up the cabbage – and heard a loud HISS! right behind me.

"Watch out, Ced!" Patchcoat yelled.

But it was too late.

SNAP!

"Yow!"

I leaped in the air as one of the geese bit me right on the bottom.

HISS!

"Yikes!" I ran for the fence and
scrambled over just in time to avoid another
painful jab in the jacksie.

I glowered at the gooseherd. "I thought
you said your geese didn't bite?"

"They don't, young master," chuckled
the gooseherd. "But those ain't my geese."

We were about to start again when the
flap to the Baking Tent opened and a dozen
contestants came out one by one, each

with a tall and very elaborate cake. They placed their cakes on a long table draped in a white tablecloth then disappeared back into the tent. The last contestant to appear was Margaret, carrying a huge charred and lopsided lump with a single cherry on top.

"Hello there again, Master Cedric!" she said, plonking the blackened, smoking object on the table. "What d'you think of me Showstopper?"

"Er, the cherry's a nice touch," I said.

"And it definitely hasn't got a soggy bottom, Maggie," said Ham, who was doing some impressive keepy-uppys with the spare cabbage.

"Showstopper?" whispered Patchcoat.

"More like a *door*stopper if you ask me!"

Margaret glared at him. "I 'eard that, Master Patchcoat!" she snorted. "If the judges wasn't coming any minute now, I'd wallop you." With that she turned and stomped back into the tent.

"Er, I think we'd better get on with our practice," I said.

I tapped the cabbage to Patchcoat, who swung at it with his foot and missed by a mile. Ham instantly let the spare cabbage drop, intercepted my shot with his left foot and neatly flicked it back to me. The spare cabbage rolled away under the table with all the cakes on it.

"Nice one!" I said. My spirits were rising. Godwit and Botolph were a bit hopeless, but at least they were keen. And their dad definitely still had star quality.

While Ham went to retrieve the spare cabbage, I tried again with the first one. This time Patchcoat got his foot to the cabbage and kicked it with all his might. Unfortunately, it shot off in the *opposite* direction to the goal.

"To you, Godwit!" I cried in alarm, as the ball flew towards the table of cakes.

Godwit didn't notice. He was busy nibbling a stray cabbage leaf and eyeing all the cakes. "Oochya!" he squawked, as the cabbage glanced off the back of his head.

Phew, at least the cakes are safe, I thought, as the cabbage rebounded high overhead.

A short distance away, the tumblers were forming a human ladder with their backs to us. The crowd cheered as the man at the top stretched out his arms in triumph.

THWOCK!

"*AARGH!*"

"*AAH! OOH!*"

The crowd scattered as the cabbage walloped the top tumbler right in the bottom, causing him to lose his balance – and making the whole human ladder collapse in a heap of arms and legs.

As if that wasn't bad enough, the cabbage rebounded again – back in the direction of the cakes!

KNIGHTMARE

"I'll catch it, Master Cedric!" hollered Botolph. He put out his arms, only for the cabbage to sail between his outstretched hands.

"Whoops!" he said.

I watched in horror as the cabbage struck the cake at one end of the table with a sickening SPLAT! The cake – or what was left of it – crumpled on to the cake next to it, which knocked over the one after that... Finally, the second-to-last cake tumbled into the cake at the very end. A large, solid, scorched, misshapen cake with a cherry on top. It teetered and tottered on the edge of the table – and then Ham's head appeared from the tablecloth, directly underneath it.

"Got it!" he grinned, holding up the stray cabbage.

"Watch out, Pa!" yelled Botolph.

It was too late. Margaret's cake finally lost its fight to stay upright and dropped off the edge of the table. Right on to Ham's head.

CLONK!

Ham sprawled senseless on the ground. We all ran to him.

He grunted as we managed to sit him up. Botolph dribbled some mead into his mouth and he began to come round.

Dazed, he stared up at us. "Wha—whazzappened?" he groaned.

"Auntie Maggie's cake fell on yer bonce, Pa!" said Botolph.

Patchcoat nudged me. "Er, I dunno about you, Ced," he said, "but I reckon it *might* just be time we disappeared."

The trio of tumblers were now getting to their feet and shaking their fists in our direction. They did NOT look pleased.

"Um – I reckon you're right," I agreed. "Come on, folks! Practice is over! Godwit, stop scoffing and give us a hand with your pa!"

"Sorry, Master Cedric!" said Godwit, who was busily filling his face with fistfuls of collapsed cake. "Waste not, want not, eh?"

He stuffed several lumps of cake into his pockets and helped us to heave his father to his very wobbly feet. Then, half leading Ham and half carrying him, we made our escape as hastily as we could into the throngs of fairgoers.

"Let's head for the Refreshments Tent," I said, once we were safely out of sight. "We can leave Ham there to recover. There's no way he's going to be able to play. And I think we'd better warn Sir Percy."

"Warn him about what, Ced?" asked Patchcoat.

"That he's going to need to find himself a new castle."

Chapter Seven
Pre-Match Panic

We pulled off Ham's sack and lay him on
a bench outside the Refreshments Tent. Just
then Sir Percy came striding out, dabbing
his mouth with a napkin.

"Sir Percy!" I called.

He looked up in alarm and instantly
switched into a rather unconvincing limp.
"*Ooh! Ahh!* Hello, Cedric," he groaned.

KNIGHTMARE

"Bother this knee! It might not clear up for days, weeks, even months. *Ooh!*"

"Your *knee*, Sir Percy?" I said. "I thought it was your *ankle*?"

"Eh? Well – um – er," he jabbered. "It's – um – it's *both*, dear boy. Yes, that's it. The sprain has – um – spread to the whole general leg area." He wafted his hand vaguely up and down his leg. "Anyway, how's my team coming along?"

Ah. It was my turn to hesitate. How could I break it to him?

"Um – well, the good news is that we do *have* a full team, Sir Percy," I said, indicating Patchcoat and the two lads. "Or rather we *did*—"

108

"Splendid, splendid!" Sir Percy interrupted. "I must make sure I get a good seat to watch you defeat Sir Roland."

"What's that, Percy?" boomed a familiar voice.

Sir Percy leaped about a foot into the air as Sir Roland and Walter swaggered out of the crowd.

"Ah, h-h-hello Roland," spluttered my master. "We were – um – just discussing – um – team tactics."

"Oh yeah?" said Sir Roland. "Sounded more like you were trying to wriggle out of playing in the match. Well, that's fine by me, Percy."

"Er, really?" said my master.

"Sure," Sir Roland went on. "Any team without the full five players at kick-off will be automatically disqualified. And you know what that means, eh, Percy? Bye-bye Castle Bombast! Hur-hur-hur!"

"Well, for your information, Roland, we *do* have a complete team," said Sir Percy indignantly. "Isn't that right, Cedric?"

There was no point in beating about the bush. I'd give him the full story later.

"Well, *yes*, Sir Percy," I said. "But only if you play, too."

Sir Percy's face fell.

"In that case, you'd better get ready for the match," said Sir Roland. "We've run out of teams to beat so it's *your* turn next. Kick-off is at three o'clock outside the village church, just past the Mad Maze. You'll find the rest of my team there, having a breather before we wipe out you lot. See you in half an hour, Percy! Hur-hur-hur!"

Guffawing loudly, Sir Roland stomped into the Refreshments Tent.

"See yah, Fatbottom," sneered Walter, eyeing my makeshift football kit. "Or should I say *Sack*bottom, he-he! I'm *so* looking forward to moving into your old room. Once I've got rid of the *smell*, of course."

Sniggering nastily, Walter disappeared after Sir Roland. I was thinking of something to shout after him when I had to step aside

to make way for a pony ridden by a filthy,
tattered urchin. He was leading a horse with
a heap of rags slung over the back.

To my surprise, the heap of rags
suddenly raised its head. "My clothes," it
whimpered. "My beautiful clothes!"

It was Sir Spencer. And the urchin was
none other than Algernon.

"Spence, old boy!" gasped my master. "Wh-what happened?"

"We just lost to Sir Roland," groaned Sir Spencer. "*That's* what. If you think *we* look bad, you should see the *rest* of the team. What's left of them."

"But what about Osbertino, your star player?" said Sir Percy.

"Um – a minor misunderstanding. Turns out he wasn't the best *keeper* in his own country. He just sold the best *kippers*. He'd never played football in his life!" Sir Spencer moaned. "I should have listened to you, Perce. No more football for me! Home, Algernon!"

"Yes, Sir Spencer," croaked Algernon.

113

"Yikes," I said, as they trotted off.
"It looks like we're *really* done for."

"Indeed," Sir Percy agreed glumly.
"I can see no way out of this wretched
match. Come along, chaps. I fear we must
prepare to face the music."

Patchcoat suddenly began racing ahead.
"I'll see you there," he called. "Something
Sir Roland said has just given me an
idea."

"What is it?" I asked.

"I'll tell you later, Ced," grinned
Patchcoat. "But if it works it might just
save Castle Bombast!"

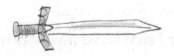

KNIGHTMARE

Team Bombast – minus Patchcoat –
made its way to the church. Sir Percy
tried to look as dignified as possible in
Ham's sack as he waved to the large
crowd that had lined the avenue of
flagpoles to watch the last match of the
May Fair tournament. But he was still in
a pretty gloomy mood.

He didn't even cheer up when his
female fans spotted him and started
chanting.

Two–four–six–eight
Who do we appreciate?
P–E–R and C and Y,
Sir Percy is our favourite guy!

As we reached the church porch a man
stepped out to meet us. He was wearing a
plain black tabard and carrying a football.

"Afternoon, Your Honour," he said to
Sir Percy. "You here for the final? I'm the
referee. Just to remind you, the church
porch is the goal. The ball must make

one circuit around the fair and back. The team that gets the ball in the porch are the winners. All means of stopping your opponents are permissible, except one."

"Whassat?" said Botolph.

"*Killing* them, of course, ha, ha!"

The referee was still laughing when the church clock struck a quarter to three.

"Kick off at three o'clock sharp," he said. "As long as Sir Roland's team is here, of course."

Sir Roland and Walter appeared at that moment. A murmur of *boos* went around the crowd.

"Ready to lose your castle, Percy?" rumbled Sir Roland. "Hur-hur-hur!"

"Just a moment, Sir Roland!" said the referee. "You can't play with just the two of you, you know."

"You trying to be funny?" snapped Sir Roland. "I told the other three to wait on that bench over... Eh?"

He stared at an empty bench at the side of the field.

"Well, they're not there now, are they, Roly old bean?" said Sir Percy, suddenly perking up. "And you know the rules, eh? Let me see – if a whole team doesn't show up at kick-off they are automatically disqualified. Isn't that right, Mister Referee?"

KNIGHTMARE

"Ah, quite so, Your Honour, quite so!"

Sir Roland glared at Sir Percy. But he also looked rather worried. "Walter, go and find the others," he barked. "They'll get extra guard duty for this!"

"Yes, Sir Roland," whined Walter, scuttling off. "Right away, Sir Roland."

Patchcoat sidled up to me. "D'you know something, Ced?" he muttered. "I've got a hunch Walter *won't* find the rest of his team in a hurry."

"So *that's* what you were up to!" I gasped. "How did you do it?"

"Easy, Ced," grinned Patchcoat. "I told them that Sir Roland wanted to see them for an urgent meeting about tactics. In there."

119

He pointed to the circular wooden enclosure nearby.

"The Mad Maze!"

"Got it in one, Ced. I reckon they'll find their way out in ooh, I dunno – a couple of hours? Oh, and one of them left these on the bench. Too small for me but they might be your size, Ced."

From under his sack tunic he pulled out – a pair of proper football boots.

A smile crept across my face, as I pulled off my shoes and tried on 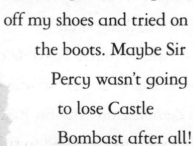 the boots. Maybe Sir Percy wasn't going to lose Castle Bombast after all!

Chapter Eight
Match Mayhem

By the time the church clock said five to three, Sir Percy was cheerfully signing autographs for his fans and bragging about his footballing skills.

"And of course I'm a *demon* dribbler," he boasted. "*Such* a shame I shan't be able to demonstrate. But Sir Roland's team are obviously too terrified to turn up!"

KNIGHTMARE

Sir Roland's glare could have demolished a castle. He looked even less pleased when Walter reappeared, apparently empty-handed.

"Dear, dear," said my master, winking at his fans. "It rather looks as if Sir Roland will be disqualified. *Very* unsatisfactory to be declared champions without playing the match. Well, I suppose one must *reluctantly* accept the situation."

Then a grin spread across Sir Roland's face as Walter whispered something in his ear. *Uh-oh.*

"Not so fast, Percy," he chuckled. "Walter here has found me some *substitutes*. Here they come now!"

KNIGHTMARE

My master's face fell about a million miles as three athletic-looking guys pushed through the crowd. My heart sank. They looked all too familiar.

"I thought our chaps might be practising near the Baking Tent," smirked Walter. "When I got there I bumped into some *rather* cross tumblers."

Tumblers? Yikes!

"They volunteered to join our team," Walter went on. "Something about getting their own back on a bunch of morons who couldn't play football for toffee. Can't think *who* they were talking about, can you, Sackbottom?"

Before I could answer, the referee

glanced at the clock. Two minutes to three. "Right, chaps!" he declared. "Almost time to start. The new team gets to kick off. I take it from your fans that you're the captain, Your Honour?"

The crowd fell silent as the referee plonked the ball at Sir Percy's feet.

Sir Percy stared at it in dismay. But then his face switched to a strangely fixed grin. "Oh, ha, ha, ha! Silly me!" he laughed, pulling the sack off over his head. "I've just realized that it's *utterly* ridiculous to try and run all the way round the fair in my armour. I shall just nip into the church and remove it."

"Shall I help you, Sir Percy?" I said.

"Otherwise you'll miss the start of the match."

"What? Oh! Ah! No, no, no, no, no," he said. "No need, dear boy, no need. I shall, er, manage very well on my own. As deputy team captain, *you* can have the great honour of kicking off the match. But don't worry! I shall catch up with you – um – er, *shortly!*"

With a quick wave at his fans, Sir Percy skipped up the steps into the church. Something told me I wouldn't be seeing him again until after the match was well and truly over. I was just thinking, *Thanks a million, Sir Percy*, when the clock struck three and a loud cheer went up from the crowd lining the course.

I looked nervously from Team Bombast to our opponents. Apart from weedy Walter I was facing a monstrous mass of muscle. It looked like I wouldn't have a castle to sleep in that night.

Oh well, I thought. *Here goes!*

I kicked the ball as hard as I could.

The match had begun!

KNIGHTMARE

The crowd roared as the ball sailed over
Sir Roland's head. It landed several metres
behind him, and instantly Sir Roland and
the tumblers were charging towards it.
They definitely had the edge in size and
power. But Botolph was surprisingly nippy,
and I suddenly saw him streaking past me
and dodging between Sir Roland and one
of the tumblers.

"Yay! Go, Botty, go!" yelled Godwit.

Botolph had almost reached the ball when one of the tumblers grabbed him by the sack and yanked him off his feet. He fell on his bottom with a squawk.

"Unfair, ref!" I cried.

The referee shook his head. "Sorry, lad," he said. "It's not against the rules."

Sir Roland charged into the gap and bent down to grab the ball. But then someone dodged under his great hairy mitts and managed to scoop it up. It was Patchcoat!

Sir Roland gave a roar and tried to seize hold of him, but Patchcoat sped off, with Sir Roland and his team in hot pursuit.

KNIGHTMARE

"Aargh!" yelped Patchcoat.

The crowd moaned "Oooh!" and
"Shame!" as he sprawled on the ground.
Walter had scuttled out of nowhere and
tripped him up. With a cackle of glee,
Wartface snatched the ball and shot off.

"That must be a foul this time, ref!"
I cried. But the ref shook his head again.

"Play on!" he said.

"Don't 'ee worry, Master Cedric, I'll get
'im!" cried Godwit, who was huffing
and puffing along some way behind me.
I glanced over my shoulder to see him stop
at a nearby food stall.

"I'll pay you later!" he said, grabbing
a large custard pie.

KNIGHTMARE

"Hey! This is no time to stop for a snack!" I said crossly.

But Godwit didn't eat the pie. He closed one eye, took careful aim and hurled it with all his might. It span through the air – and hit Walter on the head with a very satisfying SPLAT! Walter gave a loud squawk and dropped the ball.

"Crackin' shot, Goddo!" cried Botolph.

"Wow!" I said. "Why didn't you tell me you could throw?"

"'Ee never asked, Master Cedric," said Godwit. "Back home I'm village pie-tossing champion!"

Patchcoat was back on his feet and had picked up the ball before Sir Roland and the tumblers could reach him. "Can't catch me!" he laughed.

"That's what you think, sunshine," cried one of the tumblers. "Allay-OOP!"

There were gasps from the crowd as the tumbler leaped into the air, turned a somersault and landed perfectly in front of Patchcoat.

"Oof!"

Patchcoat careered straight into the tumbler and dropped the ball.

With his heel, the tumbler neatly tapped the ball sideways to Sir Roland. Sir Roland was preparing to give it an almighty kick when he spotted a short, round figure hurtling towards him at incredible speed – Godwit!

Sir Roland was so astonished he mistimed the kick and sent the ball too high. The crowd groaned as it landed on the roof of a tall and colourful pavilion, rolled down to the edge – and stayed there.

"Blimey," I said. "Talk about putting a spurt on, Godwit. I'd never have guessed you could run so fast!"

"I'd never have guessed he could run *at all*," chuckled Patchcoat.

"I had to," said Godwit. "Sir Roland was about to tread on that bit o' pie."

He picked up a splattered lump of custard pie and popped it in his mouth. "No point in wastin' it."

"You there!" hollered Sir Roland. "Come and get the ball down!"

"But I can't reach, Yer Honour!" said Godwit. "It's too high up!"

"Sorry, son," said the referee. "The player who loses a ball has to retrieve it."

"But *he* didn't lose it," I pointed out. "Sir Roland did."

Sir Roland glared at me.

I didn't fancy getting into an argument with Sir Roland. But, to my surprise, his own team came to my rescue.

The three tumblers stood by the side of the pavilion and grasped one another's hands to make a human cradle.

"Step in, lad," one of them said. "We'll give you a leg up."

They bent down to let Godwit step on their hands. It was then that I noticed the tumblers winking at Sir Roland.

"Wait!" I began. But it was too late.

"Three, two, one – *hup!*"

"*Waaah!*"

The tumblers catapulted Godwit high

into the air. He turned a perfect somersault, then plummeted feet first into the top of the pavilion with a resounding RRRRIP!

The impact dislodged the ball, which dropped straight into the waiting arms of Sir Roland. With a "Hur-hur!" of triumph he bolted in the direction of the livestock pens, followed by the tumblers.

"So long, sucker!" cried Walter, running off after them.

A woman pulled back the flap and poked her head out of the pavilion. She wore a bright red headscarf and big gold earrings.

"What's goin' on?" she demanded. "How am I supposed to concentrate on me crystal ball with two fat legs dangling over me?"

Godwit was wedged firmly up to his middle in the roof of the pavilion. "Don't 'ee worry, Master Cedric!" he said. "I'll explain everything. Get on after that ball!"

Chapter Nine
Cattle Kerfuffle

The three remaining members of Team
Bombast ran around the outside of the
fair, past stalls and sideshows, duck pens
and donkey rides. The spectators lining
the course cheered us on, including the
farmhands Sir Roland had defeated earlier.
Swathed in plasters and bandages, they
struck up a new version of their chant.

I'm a cowpat,
I'm a cowpat,
I'm a cowpat, yes I am!
But I'd rather be a cowpat
Than rotten Roland's fan!

Before long, most of the crowd were joining in. The chanting was encouraging, but we were more than halfway around the fair before we spotted our opponents again.

"That's funny," I said. "They seem to have stopped."

We soon found out why. A peasant was herding a bunch of cows right across their path.

"Blithering bludgeons!" barked Sir Roland.

KNIGHTMARE

"Can't your pesky animals go any faster? I've got a castle to win!"

Walter snatched the cowherd's stick and started prodding a particularly big animal right at the back of the herd.

"I'm not sure that's a good idea, Wartface," I said.

"Oh do shut up, Fatbottom," sneered Walter. "Just because you know we're going to win. Move it, you stupid cow!" He gave the animal an extra hard prod.

"Beggin' yer pardon, but that ain't a *cow*," said the peasant. "That's Buster. Me prize *bull*."

The beast turned and fixed Walter with an angry stare.

139

KNIGHTMARE

"Er, I hate to say I told you so, Walter,"
I said. "But – I told you so."

MURRRRRR!

The bull gave a great bellow and pawed
the ground. And then it started to move
towards Walter.

"Eek!" he squealed, backing off. "Help!
N-nice b-bull. I didn't m-mean to…"

But the bull only bellowed again,
lowered its head and charged.

I have never seen *anyone* move so fast.
The crowds following the match parted as
Walter fled in terror from a ton of furious
beef.

Luckily for him there was a clear path to
the maypole. With a yelp of terror, Walter

reached the pole and shimmied up it just in time to avoid a sharp pair of horns in the hindquarters. Walter didn't stop climbing until he was right at the top, just as the cowherd came up and deftly ran a rope through the bull's nose ring.

"Take that horrid beast away!" whinged Walter.

"Oh, I will, young master," said the cowherd. "When he's calmed down a little. Poor Buster's had a bit of a nasty shock, what with all that proddin'!"

"*He's* had a nasty shock?" wailed Walter. "What about *me*?"

Ignoring him, the cowherd tied the rope to the maypole then strolled back to the rest of his herd.

"Come back!" cried Walter. "You can't leave me up here!"

"I just did," called the cowherd.

Patchcoat and I fell about in stitches. But our laughter was interrupted by the

KNIGHTMARE

referee crying, "Play on!"

Sir Roland swiped the ball off one of the tumblers, who had been idly spinning it on his finger. Then, with the way ahead now clear, he drop-kicked it in the direction of the church.

"Castle Bombast, here I come, hur-hur!" he roared.

The tumblers sped off after Sir Roland. Patchcoat, Botolph and I raced after them, but try as we might, we just couldn't break through the tumblers. Each time we tried to outflank them, they swerved as a pack right in our way. It was like chasing a large, moving brick wall.

Botolph saw a sudden gap between

143

their legs. He tried to nip through, but the tumblers were too quick for him.

"Not so fast, sunshine!" One of the tumblers grabbed Botolph by the scruff of the neck, hoiked him into the air and swung him round his head as easily as a feather pillow.

"One–two–three… WHEEE!"

"*Waargh!*"

Nearby, some children were fishing for wooden fish in a large tub of water. They were rather startled when Botolph landed in their midst with a loud SPLASH!

I ran to help him out, but he shooed me away. "I'm fine, Master Cedric!" he cried. "You get on after that Sir Roland!"

I turned and resumed the chase with
Patchcoat. But the tumblers were as
solid as ever, and even further ahead.
Meanwhile, Sir Roland was now dribbling
the ball closer and closer to the church.

Patchcoat and I had just about given up
hope when suddenly someone shot out of the
crowd ahead of us. They barrelled into the
line of tumblers, knocking them over like
skittles.

It was Margaret!

"Any chance of a game, Master Cedric?"
she hollered, as I caught her up. "I 'eard
what 'appened from poor old Ham.
Couldn't stand by and let Sir Roland win,
could I?"

"Thanks, Margaret!" I said. "I hereby declare you a substitute! Oh, and I'm sorry about your cake."

"Eh? Cake's fine, Master Cedric," said Margaret. "Cherry fell off, that's all. Come on. Let's finish this match!"

The tumblers were soon back on their feet. As Margaret, Patchcoat and I charged after Sir Roland they caught us up and tried to tackle us. Before long, Patchcoat was rolling on the ground clutching his ankle. I stopped to help him up but he shook his head.

"I'll live, Ced! You gotta keep going or we'll lose the castle!" he said. "And don't worry about the tumblers. I reckon

Margaret'll sort them out!"

Patchcoat was right. The tumblers soon discovered that tackling Margaret was a big mistake.

"OUCH!"

"AARGH!"

"A-YEE!"

I glanced over my shoulder to see the tumblers on the ground, too, clutching freshly walloped shins and stamped-on feet.

"That'll learn 'em!" called Margaret.

I put on a burst of speed and finally caught up with Sir Roland, but getting the ball off him was another matter. Then I had an idea. I moved in closer, forcing him over towards the poles lining the course. Sir Roland stopped dribbling and gave the ball a powerful kick, only to see it hit one of the poles. The ball glanced off the pole in my direction. Seizing my chance, I picked it up and ran for my life.

"Why, you!" Sir Roland roared in frustration. "Come back here!"

I was running flat out, but Sir Roland soon began to gain on me. There was no way I'd reach the church before he caught up.

148

KNIGHTMARE

Just when Sir Roland was so close behind me I could actually hear his teeth gnashing, I saw a coach and horses hurtling at great speed up one of the roads to the village.

To my surprise, the coach slowed down right next to us. A little old lady leaned out of the door. She was richly dressed with sharp beady eyes. And, as it turned out, a sharp tongue.

"Roland!" she cried. "Leave that child alone, you big bully!"

Sir Roland stopped dead in amazement "Eh? But—but…"

As the coach began to move off again, I realized it was heading in the direction of the church. Clutching the football, I ran up to the coach door.

"Excuse me, madam," I said breathlessly.
"Could I hitch a lift to the church?"

"Certainly, young man!" said the lady.
"Hold on tight!"

I hopped on the back as it began to pick
up speed.

"Stop!" roared Sir Roland. "That's cheating, ref!"

"Er, I'm afraid not, Your Honour," said the referee. "Any means of moving the ball are allowed, remember?"

Leaving a fuming Sir Roland far behind, the coach drove on. It had to slow down again at the church because of all the fairgoers, so I had no trouble hopping off the back.

I spotted Ham at the front of the crowd, a bit unsteady on his feet, but punching both fists in the air and beaming from ear to ear. "Go, young master, go! Bravo!"

With the cheers of the crowd ringing in my ears, I ran triumphantly through the

151

churchyard, kicking the ball as I went.
Then, when I was almost at the porch, I
skidded to a halt. A figure had just slipped
out from behind a gravestone, giving me
the fright of my life.

Sir Percy!

"Um – I'll take over from here, Cedric,"
he said. (I noticed he was still wearing his
armour. He wasn't limping either.)

Before I could say anything, Sir Percy
picked up the ball, strolled the last few
metres to the church and plonked it in the
middle of the porch – just as Sir Roland and
the referee came running up.

"Hurrah! Goal to me!" my master
declared. "I won! I won! I won!"

Chapter Ten

May Queen Mayhem

Sir Percy beamed in triumph as he signed autographs for his fans and generally took every ounce of credit for Team Bombast's unlikely victory.

"Of course, it was all entirely down to my superior tactics," he boasted. "I had the whole thing planned from the start."

Patchcoat patted me sympathetically on

the shoulder. "Never mind, Ced," he said. "The main thing is, he won his stupid bet. At least we've still got a home to go to."

"PERCY! I'd like a word with you!"

Sir Percy sputtered to a halt mid-boast and stared in disbelief. The sprightly little old lady from the coach was heading straight for him.

"Oh! A-a-aunt Hilda Matilda!" he gibbered. "How the dev— I mean, how *delightful* to see you!"

"Now then, Percy," said Lady Hilda Matilda. "What's all this nonsense about you betting your entire castle?"

"Betting my c-castle, dear Aunt?" winced Sir Percy. "I'm sure there must be some mistake?"

"Poppycock!" snapped his aunt. "Don't try spinning me one of your ridiculous yarns, Percy. I've heard *all* about it from young Roland. And I've given *him* a good talking-to for taking your bet seriously."

I glanced over at Sir Roland. To judge by the way he was rubbing his left ear, she'd given him more than just a talking-to.

"It's been the same since you were both children," sighed Lady Hilda Matilda. "Always boasting and bickering and trying to pinch each other's toys."

Sir Percy squirmed uncomfortably.

"Anyway, I called at Castle Bombast on my way here," Lady Hilda Matilda went on.

"Really, Auntie?" said Sir Percy, mustering his most innocent grin.

"Indeed, Percy. That gardener fellow of yours told me you'd *just* left for the fair." She gave my master a hard, beady stare. "In some *haste*, as it seems."

Sir Percy blushed bright pink.

"Fortunately, I was heading to the fair myself," the old lady said. "I am delighted to be this year's guest of honour. Now, I would dearly love to have a smart and noble knight to escort me. But you'll have to do. Come along!"

Sir Percy had no choice but to follow Lady Hilda Matilda as she strode off towards the middle of the fair. I saw the maypole ahead of us. The farmer had just untied his bull and was leading it away. Once he was sure it was safe, Walter slid down the pole.

"Ouch!" I heard him yelp. "I've got splinters in my bottom!"

I noticed that three more wooden thrones had been lined up at the trophy table, next to the guest of honour's.

157

"Er, what exactly are we doing, Auntie?" Sir Percy said.

"Well, I am presenting *you* with the May Fair Trophy, for a start. Though I think your clever *squire* deserves it rather more than you do."

I blushed. Sir Percy gave a fake laugh.

"Oh! Ha, ha, ha! Most amusing, Auntie. Ha, ha, ha!"

"Oh do be quiet, Percy," snorted Lady Hilda Matilda. "I am also presenting the prize for the Great May Fair Bake Off. And finally I am judging the May Queen contest," she said. "Here come the contestants now!"

A line of brightly dressed young women

was trooping into the open area of the green. The young women were looking over at my master. Too late, he realized why.

"'Ere! It's that peepin' Tom!" cried one of the women. "The one what sneaked into the Changin' Tent earlier!"

My master went pale. He went even paler when who should come jingling along behind us but – the morris dancers.

"Hey! Look, lads! There he is!"

"Percy!" snapped his aunt. "What on *earth* is going on?"

"Ah – um – I shall explain later, Auntie dearest," he said. "I, er, I think I'd better—"

"After 'im, lads!"

"After 'im, girls!"

Sir Percy spotted a gap between two pavilions and shot down it. I dived after him.

My master ducked round the back of another tent — only to find his way barred by a large wicker basket marked "Costumes".

"Excellent!" said Sir Percy. "I can hide in here."

He flung open the lid, but the basket was full.

"Bother!" he said. "But never mind, Cedric, I shall wear one of these as a disguise."

He pulled out a baggy bright green costume with what looked like wings attached to the back. Underneath it was

KNIGHTMARE

some sort of grotesque
green monster's head.
"Ah! The very thing.
It will hide my face
splendidly. Quick, help
me out of my armour!"

I hastily unstrapped him. Then
I helped him into the costume.

"Now I am in disguise I can slip back to
Prancelot and, er, discreetly make my way
home to the castle," he said. "Once I'm well
clear you can run along to my aunt and
make my excuses."

"But what shall I tell her, Sir Percy?"

"I'm sure you'll think of something, dear
boy," he said, pulling on the monster's head.

"Oh, and when you come home, don't forget to bring my armour. *And* my trophy."

Thanks a bunch, Sir Percy.

Checking the coast was clear, Sir Percy slipped out from behind the tent and headed off into the crowd, trying — and utterly failing — to look inconspicuous in the ridiculous monster costume. Once I'd lost sight of my master, I made my way back to the clearing around the maypole. As I pushed my way to the front of the crowd, there was a great round of clapping and cheering. I was just in time to see Lady Hilda Matilda placing the crown of silver flowers on the head of one of the May Queen contestants.

KNIGHTMARE

The new May Queen curtsied to the crowd and took her seat on one of the thrones at the guest of honour's table. It was then I noticed that one of the other two thrones was already occupied. By Margaret. She was beaming broadly as she clutched the Bake Off trophy!

While I was still taking it in, Lady Hilda Matilda spotted me.

"Ah! You, boy!" she said. "Where's that useless master of yours? He was supposed to be here to receive the football trophy. I've already had to delay the presentation twice."

"Um – he said he hurt his ankle, my lady," I said. Which was true. He *had* said it. About three hours ago. "And he's gone to, er, to change his dressing." Which was also true. Sort of.

"Humph," she snorted. "A likely story. But never mind," she said, with the hint of a twinkle in her eye. "If he's not here, it can't be helped. AHEM!"

She stood up and cleared her throat loudly. The crowd fell silent. "Ladies and gentlemen!" she announced. "I have great pleasure in presenting the May Fair Trophy to the winners. Kindly step forward and receive the trophy, er –" Margaret leaned over and whispered in her ear – "Master Cedric Thatchbottom and his team!"

I suddenly felt myself being pushed forward. I turned to see the beaming faces

KNIGHTMARE

of Ham, Patchcoat, Godwit and
Botolph.

"Go on, Ced!" said Patchcoat.
"We're right behind you!"

I took the trophy
from Lady Hilda Matilda and
raised it above my head. The
crowd went wild.

"Now, Master Cedric, kindly take
your seat in the remaining throne.
We mustn't delay the performance
any longer."

"Performance, my lady?"

"Indeed. The morris dancers are doing a
special dance to celebrate the crowning of
the May Queen."

As she spoke, the morrismen jingled
into view, accompanied by their musicians.
I took my seat, with the rest of Team
Bombast gathered around me, as the chief
morrisman approached the table and
bowed to the May Queen.

"My lady," he declared. "We be proud
to bring 'ee our traditional dance in honour
o' the May Queen. It depicts the triumph
of summer over winter. We present – 'The
Battle of the Dragon'!"

There were cheers as the musicians
struck up a jolly jig and the morrismen
began their dance. First, the dancers came
on dragging a – very reluctant – dragon.
Even Lady Hilda Matilda giggled when

KNIGHTMARE

the dragon kept trying to run off into the
crowd. I guessed it was all part of the show,
just like the dragon's wails of "Wah!"
and "Ouch!" and "Aargh!" as the dancers
walloped it one by one with their cudgels.
But then something occurred to me. That
dragon costume ... surely it couldn't be...

At that moment a man ran out of the crowd, dressed from head to toe in a sort of protective undershirt padded with straw.

"Sorry I'm late, lads!" he panted. "Someone nicked me dragon costume!"

"Don't worry, Seth," grinned the chief morrisman. "We found it."

"Help!" wailed the dragon again, as the dancers gave it one final wallop with their cudgels all at once. "Help! Cedric!"

Cedric? Oh dear.

"So you see, the judges *had* to give me the Bake Off prize," said Margaret, chopping a turnip in half with a single blow of her knife. "On account of my cake being the only one that survived your little practice session, Master Cedric."

"Oh well," I said. "Every cloud has a silver lining."

I filled the wooden pail I was carrying with hot water from a large cauldron hanging over the kitchen fire.

"Eh?" said Margaret sharply. "You saying I *wouldn't* have won otherwise, Master Cedric?"

"No, of course not!" I said hastily. "Your Showstopper was by far the most, er, remarkable."

"Ced's right, Margaret," grinned Patchcoat,

who was sitting at the kitchen table. "Your cake was an absolute knockout. Just ask your brother!"

Margaret glared at him. "You watch your step, Master Patchcoat," she said. "Or I'll be addin' a couple more bruises to the ones Sir Roland's lot gave you."

"Talking of bruises," said Patchcoat, changing the subject. "I wonder how Sir Percy's doing after his morris-dancing escapade?"

"A bit on the sore side, I reckon," said Margaret. "Can't think why else he'd want a bath only three months after his last one. Bloomin' waste o' water, if you ask me." She peered into the cauldron, which was almost empty.

KNIGHTMARE

The Knight's Code of Honour says that every knight has to take a bath twice a year, whether he needs one or not. And it's the squire's job to fill the bath. Which was why I'd already carried *twenty* pails upstairs to my master.

"Right, I'd better get back," I said. "Otherwise Sir Percy will start moaning about the water getting cold."

I heaved the pail upstairs to Sir Percy's chamber, where he was soaking in a large wooden bathtub.

"Ah, there you are, Cedric," he said. "I wondered where you'd got to."

"Sorry, Sir Percy," I said, as I tipped the pail of hot water into the tub.

"Aah! That's better," he sighed. "A hot bath is *just* the thing after a day of, er, strenuous sport."

"Yes, Sir Percy."

Strenuous sport? That was one way of putting it. My master sank deeper into the bath, wincing as he went. Probably something to do with the big purple bruises all over his arms, legs and shoulders.

"Gosh, those morrismen certainly gave you a good walloping, didn't they, Sir Percy?"

"A *walloping*, dear boy?" he said. "They were the gentlest of taps. I was *delighted*

when those gentlemen, er, *asked* me to join their fascinating traditional dance. I'm sure you'll agree I entered fully into the spirit of the occasion."

"Er, yes, Sir Percy." *Asked?* Dragged you kicking and screaming more like.

"Sheet, please, Cedric," said Sir Percy, carefully hauling himself out of the bath with more winces and groans. "Help me to dress and then you can empty the bath."

Once my master was dry and dressed, I filled up the pail with water and carried it downstairs — the first of many trips. Margaret was just tipping a heap of chopped vegetables into the cauldron.

"Just leave that here, Master Cedric,"

she said. "I'll empty it while you takes that spare pail by the door. It'll be quicker that way. Sooner you finishes, the sooner we can all have our supper."

"Thanks, Margaret," I said, putting down the pail. "What *is* for supper, by the way?"

"Turnip 'n' cabbage soup," she said. "Me *special* recipe. We normally only has it twice a year."

"Really?" I said. "What makes it so special?"

"It's all down to the tasty stock," she said. She picked up the pail of Sir Percy's bathwater and poured it into the cauldron. "Waste not, want not, I always say, Master Cedric!"

Coming Soon!

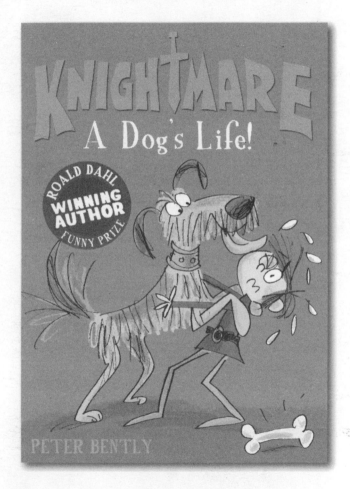